MOMENTS THAT MATTER

Vikrant Kelkar & Usha Sandhyana

Made with ❤ on the Notion Press Platform

www.notionpress.com

In loving memory of Our friend, philosopher and guide Devnish Uikey. We all miss you a lot.

I extend my deepest appreciation to my wife, Ankita Phatak, and brother, Sushant Kelkar, for their steadfast support and encouragement, which played a pivotal role in bringing this book to completion. Katyayani Bopardikar, your candid feedback and constructive criticism helped me a lot.

To DC Gang, Chinmay, and all my close friends and loving family members, your motivation and belief in me fuelled my determination to pursue my dream of completing this first book which is a crucial step in my writing journey enabling me to understand the nuances of this world.

I am sincerely grateful for each one of you who played a role, big or small, in this creative endeavour. Your contributions have made a significant impact, and I am truly blessed to have such a supportive circle.

With Warm Regards,
Vikrant Kelkar

I always wanted to write a book but it wouldn't been possible without my supporting pillars - My Husband, Family and Friends.

As I reflect on the completion of my book, I am overwhelmed with gratitude for the unwavering support Minesh Chand Meena (My Husband) has provided throughout this journey. Your encouragement, understanding, and patience have been my pillars of strength.

Devender Bhansali, Inderpreet Singh my dear friends who took the time to read and appreciate my work, your kind words have been a source of inspiration. Your encouragement fuels my passion for storytelling.

To my family, your love and encouragement have been my constant motivation. Your belief in my dreams has made this journey more special.

This book is not just my creation; it's a culmination of the support, encouragement, and love from each one of you. Thank you for being a part of this incredible chapter in my life.

With heartfelt gratitude,
Usha Sandhyana

Nikhil Tayade, our Manager - Author of Coffee Table Stories, you are inspiration for both of us. Your guidance and encouragement throughout this journey have been an invaluable contribution. We always had an example to look forward to and maintain our belief in exploring ourselves.

Prologue

Life gets pretty busy for all of us, and finding time is tough, especially for folks who love reading or writing compared to watching videos or reels. But hey, that shouldn't stop us from enjoying our passions. That's why I came up with the idea of putting together a bunch of short stories—it's like a warm-up before diving deeper into all the other long-term ideas clustered in my head.

On this writing adventure, I met Usha, a super talented and emotionally charged writer. We teamed up to blend our experiences and create a compilation. We both believe in little moments from our daily lives which go unnoticed but hold some important lessons for all of us. We started jotting down such examples, and building up on them with our imagination and creativity in order to give our beloved readers a closer experience and then also a few points to ponder.

Our goal? Make it easy for readers to grab a chapter during a quick break, enjoy the story, and leave that break with a positive thought. The prologue is your ticket to join us on this journey, where we share these short, refreshing tales.

Contents

From the Porch

It was evening, around 4 in winters, in a small town with a population of 20 thousand in Kansas. There was still time before it got dark, and I used to sit for a good amount of time on the front wooden porch. A small yard separated this porch from the town road. In the latter half of my 70s, I had plenty of time to spend with my pen and paper. We had a small tea table and another chair for her. There was no third chair there. We could have gotten one if there had been anyone else, but we rarely had visitors, and most of them were from this town, stopping by while on the way to groceries or something.

It was getting cooler. I was waiting for my coffee and struggling to pen my thoughts properly. She came late that day, around 15 - 20 minutes. She used to brew coffee for both of us after waking up from the post-lunch nap, and then we used to sit there together, watching a few people pass by. We observed the intermittent breeze move the lush green leaves of the trees around, making a sweet sound as it happened.

Sometimes she used to get her puzzles on the tea table and keep solving them for hours while I wrote. Sometimes we used to talk about our memories and then get lost in thoughts. She was beautiful. She had wrinkles on her face, and her skin had become a little looser, but I tell you she still looked beautiful with gray wavy hair. She enjoyed her daily chores, never complained, and woke up daily with the same enthusiasm I saw in her during our initial days.

I met her in Walmart probably 50 years ago, or around that period. She was a store manager, and I liked her energy, her empathy for her team, and passion to serve her customers. I liked it so much that I quickly became her regular customer and then asked her out one day. She was alone in town as her family moved back to their farm in a small old town near Buffalo. She chose to stay back for her job, and probably it was destined for us to meet. She helped me settle down in the town, and I enjoyed helping her in whatsoever way I can. And then we got married and moved together. What a beautiful time it was. How different that age is. We talk to strangers, engage with unknowns, get into relationships, take risks, move in together, and commit to each other for a lifetime. Sometimes it works, and otherwise, there is a life full of sorrow. For us, it worked great. We knew what we have and what we can get. We enjoyed our initial years exploring every other town around, sometimes even till Missouri, Arkansas, and Oklahoma. Spending time beside the lakes reading, walking through museums, enjoying the southern food and comfort. When we are 30, we start feeling older, but when we look back now, it is such a small step.

"Would you like another round of coffee, darling?" She asked, and I nodded. I was quite in the flow of thoughts. She came back and started, "You seem to be silent today." "I thought you would start with your puzzles and then just keep being a silent listener in the conversation," I said. "No, I am not doing puzzles this week. What thoughts are you into?" "I was writing a story and started wandering about our initial days in the town. I still enjoy remembering the time when our kids played in the backyard and I put up a tent for them," I spoke.

She took a sip of coffee, "And then they stayed in the tent the whole day some weekends. Now they are living in their big houses in cities. Coming once a year or two to tell their stories to their children."

"Time goes by. Life keeps moving on. As we get older, before we get ready to retire from this world, there is a new world created by our young ones and ready to walk a similar path. I remember our kids getting out of school and then to college. I remember them working hard to get into better places and their happiness as they got good jobs in cities like they had dreamt of. And then leaving us two in this small little town with the memories of the past 50 years. We never felt sad as they moved to pursue their careers just because it was good for them," I said.

She continued, "Life is to be lived that way. We can have only our limited share of love towards anyone. Not less than that. Not more than that. After that, you have to let them go. To allow them to take better shape. To explore their destinies."

It was a deep thought. I agree we need to let them go after a certain point. So they also let us go. Happily. After we are done with our time on earth. Leaving all beautiful memories behind. Memories of our childhood, exploring this beautiful town together, falling in love, the birth of our kids, and then their growing up, moving away and then days and days of spending time on this porch with this beautiful old woman. That's how life is beautiful.

_ Vikrant _

A Deep Void

A girl named Diya was working in Mumbai and trying to understand her life with daily hustle of running world. She belonged to a rural area where currently her mother was leaving alone as she had lost her father 3 years back and mother was leaving with his memories and continuing her daily routine life.

One day she thought to visit her mother for couple of days and while returning her mother said she also would like to come with Diya to Mumbai. Diya was surprised and excited at same as she never thought her mother would want to leave that place where she spent her whole life.

They both came back to Mumbai, rented a house and started leaving together but by now Diya had adopted Mumbai life (Doing things your own pace) and mother had habit of getting at 5am and doing chores as designated time and each lifestyle was getting in their way but they tried accommodating to one another schedule and ways of life.

Slowly Diya taught her mother how Mumbai life is different than her village and mother taught her some things which should not be forgotten wherever you are. Their relation got strong day by day and they started talking as friends; sharing thoughts, life experiences, hidden stories about each other and that's where Diya revealed her mother that she is in relationship with a boy named Rohit. she was sure that her mother will be furious and would not want her to pursue this but her mother's reaction was very contradictory and they spent night talking about guy, how they met, what Diya like about Rohit and what she doesn't like, what's future hold for them and mother insisted that she want to meet Rohit.

Diya told night conversation to Rohit, and he was also very happy that her mother was being so openminded and wanted to meet him. Rohit was in another city and came to meet her mother and they all gelled up very nicely. This continued for year and day came where Diya and Rohit had huge fight and it continued for days and it reaches to a place where relationship was getting over. Diya became very sad but couldn't share anything with mother and kept her felling inside her, mother suspected that something is wrong, and she called Rohit if he knew anything, but he said everything is normal may be some stress of work.

Diya had told Rohit that she will tell her mother in her own time, and he should not say anything to mother, and he kept the promise. (By now they had broken up)

A week later Diya was talking to her mother about her father and sweet memories she holds of him like how papa used to support mummy and do small things for her to make her happy, make food while mother used to be angry and shout at kids just to make her mother think that kids are being punished for bad behaviour but gave money to kids to be involved in his plan and act with him.

This whole conversation brought tears to her mother's eyes and at that moment Diya realized that how long her parents have been together, grew together since their 20's, stood together in all situation and loved each other without any condition and it made her cry while imagining that how big void her mother has after his demise and no one can fill it up.

Diya thought how sad, helpless, hopeless she was feeling after she broke with her boyfriend which was only a relation of 2 -3 years but what her mother had lost is incomparable and unbearable. She knew how strong her mother is and how hard she is trying to fill that gap which included leaving village and memories far away and engage herself in new things. She hugged her mother and made promise to herself that her mother is going to be her first priority and only true love which would never leave and will help her mother to become stronger and more independent in all possible way.

Now her mother is staying with her from last 10 years and they laugh together, live together, make fun of each other and Diya did not send her mother to village even after getting married. She kept the promise of keeping her mother her priority and she never felt low, sad, lonely after that moment as she knew her sadness and loss is way smaller than what her mother had gone through, and it made her a strong girl.

_ Usha _

Parallel journeys

6 PM. Almost 100 km from Hyderabad. Somewhere near Zaheerabad I am having a refreshing tea at a roadside Dhaba. Dusk is falling. And it is my first long bike ride. A little afraid I am now rather than being excited. Nothing planned. Had packed my bag in half an hour with whatever important stuff that came to my mind. It was my inexperienced estimate that led me to think I will reach my destination by 11 at night. People here at the tea stall are suggesting that I drive for another hour and search for a shelter nearby. They are weakening my will.

It is getting colder outside. I am not aware of the road conditions on the way. There are thousands of multi-directional thoughts popping up into my mind every second. Not wanting to rest more and waste my time after finishing up my tea, I put up my headsets and got over the roads again. It was my favourite playlist and the song was "Dooriyan hai Zaroori, Zaroori hai yeh Dooriyan", from Break ke baad, as I clearly remember.

80 Kph. I could not go beyond this due to oncoming headlights. I seriously don't know how and why I am doing this. I have never been this crazy before. For a first timer like me, this is a huge thing.

I was feeling like going through a dark tunnel having no idea of what it will be like after the tunnel ends and light allows me to have a look at the clear picture.

Ankita. Her thought was more prominent. The girl I was going to see for the first time. Will we both like each other? Will we be comfortable? Will she be like the picture of her I have in my mind? And many more thoughts in the list.

It was mid-December when we started talking to each other. I got her number from some random social networking group and pinged her. I don't remember how long she took to reply to me back but she did. She was in Pune and me in Hyderabad. We started with a huge difference in our attitudes. I started with my flirty way of chatting and she opposed my way with the same intensity. I had my philosophy and she had her thinking. I even challenged her that a day will come when she won't be strong enough to oppose any of my flirty words. And she opposed this statement too.

The next day she was traveling to her native and had enough time to spend on a call. 1.00 PM to 10.00 PM used to be my office working hours. My cell rang at 9.00 PM. It was her number. She said she left Pune. I left the office at 10.00 and gave her a call from my regular tea stall. We decided to talk over the call once I reached home. It was our first long duration call. We almost had a long 3-hour conversation that day. The story continued for the next few days when she was at home.

In my mind, she was a simple girl. Having a defensive way of decision making and living in the centre of her comfort zone. I was, in most of the cases, opposite. We both were regularly having our long duration night conversations daily. We used to discuss our likes and dislikes. Somehow, I felt she had a rather different set of thought structure and I generally appreciate someone having uniqueness in his thoughts. Borrowed thoughts are the ones I hate in the first place. We used to talk till 3 or sometimes even 4 in the morning. I really don't remember what topics we covered in those discussions prominently. But the psychological agreement with each other grew.

We also discussed a couple of times that there are chances we may fall in love. But we both had our experiences and agreed upon trying our best not to fall for each other.

Heart, sometimes, is like a balloon freely hovering in the air. Neither we want to pull it back nor we want to set it free.

We were expressing to each other the reasons why we should have our separate paths. But, I know, both, inside our hearts were having that mysterious pull that was going slowly uncontrollable.

It all tilted from not wanting to fall in love slowly towards let's see after we meet each other personally. And still we were unaware. Yeah! It's kind of funny. We started discussing expectations we had from our life partners. We had decided to meet on 27th May, exactly 23 years after the day she was born. We both were excited and planned a lot about our first meeting.

But eventually we started getting closer to each other and I wanted a chance to meet her before getting completely involved. I asked her to arrange a Skype call but she was not that familiar with these things and was also not having a fast-working internet connection. She had a cousin in Pune and she said she will be visiting for his marriage in mid of January. I asked her to spare some time for me when she is in Pune. It was possible for me to travel to Pune and spend a weekend. But she was hesitant. It was obviously out of her comfort zone. And telling a lie to meet me outside was not in her policies, at that time.

As the time passed, I saw her pushing ahead with all my efforts to meet her. I was not fine with that. It was Friday afternoon when I pinged her on WhatsApp asking her time on the coming weekend. And she gave many reasons. "There is this function at home, no one will allow me to go outside etc." I kept mum. Again, at night we had a long and deep conversation which confused me about where things were going. The next afternoon I made up my mind and called her. She repeated the earlier mentioned reasons. I convinced her that if my boss approves my leave for Monday, I am sure to come. I was fine even if she gave me a single hour out of those 2 days. Somehow, she was convinced. I readily called up my boss and without a word he said OK. It was surprising.

Now my heart started beating faster. It was 2 in the afternoon. I conveyed this plan to Pinu & Sam, my younger brothers and Prakash who lived in Pune so as to make some close people aware, just in case. Started putting stuff into my back. Wore a jacket. Charged my cell for a couple of minutes. Put up shoes. Selected the playlist and plugged in the earpieces. I informed her that I will be traveling, but she didn't ask how, and due to the low battery, I would be putting the phone on flight mode.

I did some calculations. It was 500 km. Nonstop ride at 80 Kph will get me to the destination at around 11.

But, in reality, it took me around an hour to get out of the city after filling up my tank due to heavy traffic. And now It is 7 PM and I have just left Zaheerabad 15 mins back after that tea break. With time traffic is getting sparse. Shall I take a halt somewhere in Omega which is still 100 Km ahead. I am dubious. After some

30-40 Km I was beneath the board that said - "Welcome to Karnataka".

Either way I was in two states.

The road started getting worse. Potholes and diversions. I removed my glasses. I was without any riding gears. Not even a helmet. Facing dust and headlight tortures I was counting the kilometres.

I was still happy to see Dhaba intermittently giving me an option to stop whenever required and also a feeling of safety. I crossed Humnabad and later reached Omerga. 213 out of 530 km. Feeling hungry I thought of having something at this place from where the next sign board was visible which said -"Thanks for visiting Karnataka".

I called up Prakash telling him the situation. He did an approximate estimation saying it will take another hour for me to reach Solapur further, which the road is awesome. I had 'Mirchi bhaji' at the place and a round of tea.

Back on the roads. It was chilling cold now. The cold breeze together with the oncoming lights for a first-time rider without glasses and helmet won't allow speeding more than 60 kph maximum. And to my surprise the road added to the thrill.

It was a lonely road now. Neither a Dhaba, nor any source of light, not a single vehicle I was able to see. It was sheer dark and I was feeling like midnight even though the time was around 9.30. Earlier thousand thoughts I had were now multiplied to billions. "No dacoits won't come into the way so soon.It is not even midnight," I told myself. "On both sides there is a sort of sparse jungle, but I won't be harmed by animals till I am in speed". "But what if my bike fails for any reason".

And this 'But' almost killed me.

I tried removing my earpieces but It made me feel lonely so I put them on again. I started remembering Lord Krishna and his flute. I started thinking about his time. How he would have managed his herds in such darkness. How thc melody of his flute would have enchanted the people. The thoughts made me a little stable and then a little bit more.

I was shivering with cold but felt relaxed when, after a long time, I saw some lights scattered at a distance. I have spotted a city. After around half an hour I realized I was in Solapur. I was dying hard for a break but then thought of having it when the so-called awesome road started. I saw a board pointing towards the right for Pune. I stopped at the first Dhaba when it was 11 and had 2 rounds of tea there. It was a big 6 lane further and in a good condition. I thought of going up to 100 kph but again the cold. Tembhurne, Indapur, Bhigwan, Yavat and yes, I have crossed the last toll.

At around 4 am I saw Prakash waving from the roadside walkway. I switched off the engine and gave him a hug.

We slept at 6 in the morning and my phone rang at 8. It was her call. She was available only at 11 AM and only for an hour. Meeting point was a distance of 2 hours from where I was staying. I got up, got ready and started around 9, after a 5-hour break from the ride. In my first meeting with her my eyes were all red and hair helmet shaped from the long night ride.

It was a brief meeting. I meet her again next month in Pune and that is a different story altogether. Many such meetings happened in the coming months, many fights, many possibilities of getting to separate paths, many ups and downs in the relationship but eventually we got engaged and then married after a year.

It made me believe in one thing much more.

If something is really bound to happen, destiny will not allow it to deviate. You may not find real logic on why things happened. You may get all the energy in the world above and beyond your limits when the Almighty wants to get things done from you and when not, you may not be able to do even what you are skilled at. Such situations make me humble and those who have experienced anything similar will definitely agree with me.

(Do not hesitate to share your stories with us and we would be glad to connect and know you more)

_ Vikrant _

Forgiveness

It started with any Regular day of working person life. Getting up early for a run or Gym, walking back home with list of things asked by mother or kids and connecting with friends, society elders for quick chit chat but thinking about being late for breakfast and important presentation to deliver with huge audience.

Entering in house with chaos of kids getting ready, parents listening devotee songs on high volume, maid trying to rush her day through leaving the corner uncleaned but midst of this you do not have many choices and till now Riya had understood that acceptance is the key to feel happy and stress free.

Moving on with day she completed her daily chores and gets into a conversation with husband to get some work lined up for weekend, husband on other hand was under some stress of office work and it made him neglect the conversation unconsciously and kept saying hmm, hmm, hmm for everything Riya spoke and she understood that he is not listening just hearing. Riya was holding hair dryer in her hand and situation seems daunting to her, but she wanted to be calm and quiet for her day ahead and did not want to get into arguments. She said then all settled for weekend and will have fun. Suddenly he said what fun, what are we doing? I wasn't even listening to your blabber about weekend, I am focusing on my important work at office not like your office. *"Not Like you"* shook her temper and took it to 9th cloud with full lightening feeling.

He was already into hustle of his day and did not realize what he has done. Riya could not hold her anger and said what do you mean by *"Not Like you"*, do you think you are the only one who is working. I am even working at home, and you only work for office, and it led to an uninvited fight in that moment, they started telling everything they could remember from past incidences and using high pitch to convey the messages to each other. They were so late and in hustle to office but did not realize anything during this fight and continued to remind each other of old time where she thinks he did not do good and he did the same by reminding every time when she wasn't right .

In-between of this heated conversation Riya looked at her phone and saw their was 5 missed called from her colleague with whom she used to travel to office . He used to live near by and they use to carpool to avoid unnecessary .Her colleague was getting frustrated being unsure about to wait for her or move ahead without her . She called him back stating that she will be downstairs in 2 mins. She took the lunch bag and laptop and slammed door on his face . Her husband was still inside the home and thought to give it sometime before he leaves to office. Leaving the conversation around the dialogues they moved ahead with own routine and left for office.

He was riding bike to the office and thinking about what happened in morning. Each and every dialogue was going back and forth in his mind and he was not able to understand why they got frustrated and started shouting. He kept thinking again and again and could not find even a single thing which was really a big issue to be fighting but unfortunately they end up fighting .

Riya also reached office and completely dived into her important meeting which was in couple of hours. She even forgot about the arguments and her temper as it didn't even exist for that moment. It was her presentation for During her presentation delivery she was explaining the importance of accepting the situation with consequences but more importantly forgetting the bad side of incidence if we need to heal / forgive someone 100% and it reminds her morning conversation with husband and she realized that bringing old incidents in today's conversation shows that both had accepted few thing but not forgotten how it made them feel and that essence is still present within them somewhere.

She completed her presentation and called her husband to share what she had realized and made a pact that they will work on not bringing the old incidences and make things worse in present.

_ Usha _

Soulmates

It happens between us sometimes. We fight, we argue. Sometimes I am lazy; sometimes she is arrogant. I left home full of anger this morning to get the groceries I promised my wife yesterday.

I walked into the mart, opened up my Google Keep notes, and started putting stuff into my basket, walking through the aisles on a Sunday afternoon. As I was walking through the groceries, I saw a girl picking up something from the floor and putting it into her basket. She was facing towards the other side. A sudden shiver ran down my spine. She seemed familiar. I noticed her swinging hair as she stood up and walked ahead. Jeans and a black top. I continued my search for veggies in the aisle, but curiosity caught me, and my eyes were giving a glance periodically. I thought she also saw me for a millisecond while picking up her stuff. Is she the one whom I am guessing? How can she not recognize me? Probably, I am wrong. I wished I was wrong.

And then, after walking a few steps, she stopped and started picking up something else hurriedly. I could see her side, and I was damn sure she was Aditi. Probably, she also saw but was avoiding it. Probably she was afraid or confused. There was a storm running inside me as well, but I kept calm and walked towards her. She slowly turned as I walked closer. Damn! The fragrance made me nostalgic. I think the last time I saw her was years ago. As our eyes met, I traveled back to the time we first met. I got lost for a moment in those piercing black eyes, sharp nose, and her beautiful face and then brought myself to senses. With a casual smile, we acknowledged each other. In that awkward silence, many stories flashed at the speed of light. I remember how we started getting closer to each other after we met in the office. I remembered our late-night calls, the amount of care she showed, always ready for long evening walks, going out to movies together. I remembered how feelings started growing towards her and our first beautiful date. I remembered her getting angry and crying when I forgot to inform her about going out of town for a few days and other such small things. I remembered how I consoled her until I saw a smile on her face. I remembered our winter bike rides, watching movies together, and our sweet little fights. I remembered that day when she came drenched in rain, and I felt so worried about her. I remembered the view of those sparkling droplets on her hair. I had proposed to her for marriage that day, and yes, she rejected. Straightaway. My heart went standstill. I could not understand which version of her to believe. I mustered my courage and thought of leaving the city to start afresh. I remember she cried on my shoulders for hours, and I said nothing. As I left the city, I removed all her contacts and links, and we never met again ever after. And now she is standing here in front of me after all those years. Silent.

I so wanted to ask her why she fooled around with me, but words seemed to be powerless. My eyes were filled with complaints and hers with a million questions. Both were about to saturate. We became aware of the surroundings for a while and came back to the present, exchanged a formal smile, and I walked away. I did not bother looking back at her again.

As I drove back home, I remembered the fight with my wife and that she was waiting for me to come back with groceries. I might have missed quite a few things on the list, probably. But I had learned a lot about my wife. She was the one who walked the real journey with me. She accepted me when I had practically nothing and stood by me through all my struggles. She is the one who resists all my anger and accepts me the way I am. She is a strong support in whatever things I plan to do. She is my soulmate. I so wanted to thank her for all that she did after coming into my life. As I went home and saw her, words again seemed to be powerless. I went towards her and hugged her affectionately.

_ Vikrant _

A long Flight

An entrepreneur who was smart, quick, knowledgeable, intelligent and capable of taking steps needed to take business to height. She was one of the people who speaks to think, and many times called as chatterbox, but it didn't bother her. She has accepted that she is this way and would not change for anyone neither would look to adapt being quieter.

Mostly she used to travel with her colleagues, friends and family but one day she was travelling alone. No one around her bothered to be interested in sharing thoughts and discussing new ideas or anything. She started looking into the mini-TV provided into plane and engaged herself there. Her flight was of 10hrs, and she watched tv, read book, slept for some time but it was just 4hrs completed and she had another 6 hours to go.

Passenger sitting beside her was noticing her and he could see how furious she seems, but he kept quiet and didn't say anything. She started walking here and there and all people who ever said that she is chatter box started coming into her mind and she started thinking it might be true and she never accepted the truth. She sat down on her seat and started introspecting herself. She felt like she was back in time and realizing each and every scenario where she denied to be that person.

Another passenger again looked at her and he found that something has changed, she seems calm, quiet and little bit unsettled. He kept noticing for some time and it thought to check on her and asked her if she's, okay? Does she need anything? She nodded her head and said "No". She was juggled up with all the thoughts going on in her mind and she was somewhere convinced that everybody was right, and she was wrong. She didn't even feel like talking to her neighbour; in normal scenario's she wouldn't have lost this chance where someone is trying to talk, and she remained silent.

He did not want to invade her privacy and kept quiet, but he knew something is bothering her from the change in her facial expression. It seems like situation has turned the corner as he wanted to talk to her, but she didn't seem interested. He waited for 5 min and tried again to talk to her, he said you seems upset or concerned about something, Is all good? She said "Yes "a little and not sure what to do. He said if you are okay, we can talk about it, may be that helps and as per her true nature she could not control herself and started sharing what she was thinking and going through.

He listened to her calmly and was thinking it's not a big concern, but it seems to her right now as she has all mingled up in her head right now. After listening to everything he said, Can I ask you something? She says "Yes". Do you have this thought normally or is it for first time?

She- First Time and may be because I do not have anyone near me, and I feel bored or unusual situation. He was happy that at least she is near to the reason of why she is feeling this way, but she hasn't figured it out. It's okay to feel this way, it happens when you fly alone or travel alone for linger time, you get multiple thoughts which may be not right, or which may be not big but seems to us at that point of time. So, why don't you try watching TV to distract your mind and see how you feel after some time.

She wasn't happy with advice, but she wasn't feeling like talking as well and though tot be watch something and be quiet for some time. She started going through the Movies/Shows /Cartoon on the Mini TV but couldn't decide then he Jumped in and said let me suggest you one. Give it a chance and see if you like it. She again didn't say anything and kept quiet. He started a movie which had picturization but no sound, it was mute movie.

She felt so frustrated, what kind of movie is this and how am supposed to understand it. She just wanted him to keep quiet and leave her alone and for that she kept quiet and didn't utter a word about how she is feeling. She thought she will just keep the TV on and later on Sleep may be, but she did not release but after couple of minutes her mind was totally busy into understanding the action & words people were muttering without voice. Around after 10min she realized that she actually understood the stories/scenario and became so happy that she removed her headphone (She didn't even realize that she is using headphone for movie which doesn't have voice) and nudged that guy to tell him that she is actually understating little bit of it and happiness and Joy was back on her face.

He started smiling and told her to watch the complete movie and tell him story at the end.

She was suddenly full of joy and continued watching the movie. An hour later she finished the movie but didn't feel like talking to anybody. Passenger was still noticing her and gave her couple of mins to relax and complete her chain of thoughts.

Suddenly she realized that she has to tell him the story and she nudged him to tell the story, she took around 15mins to complete the story and he asked what you learned from it. She started talking about how without words also we can express her view and convey our message. It was one of the ways to look at this and she thought this was because her mind was going around talking less. He asked again, did you learn anything else, and she started thinking that she might have missed anything in movie and nodded her head as NO.

He said it doesn't matter how one conveys their message, talking too much or being quiet as that's' not the important quality. Sometime people "Think to Speak" or "Speak to Think" and its every individual choice and that's not the important quality, Quality is to understand what each and every individual wants to speak with their way for speaking and understanding this movie shows that you have that capability/Quality of understanding everyone and you should be focusing on that ...

Do not pressurize yourself with what others says but be confident on knowing yourself.

She was awestruck by listening to this and surprised that she never thought from that view and suddenly her focus shifted to how she listens to everyone in business. understand their view and able to communicate with everyone in their own way. She felt relax, calm and smile on her face she said "THANKYOU" to the neighbour and spent her rest of journey peacefully with satisfaction.

_ Usha _

A Night to Remember

It was around 11.30 PM. We left Madhapur, passed Cyber towers, took a right from Kothaguda, and headed towards Old Mumbai Highway. It was our Friday routine. We had developed this addiction to riding around at night for about a year. It started slowly but grew. Initially, there was fear of unknown places, language barriers, but it transformed into curiosity, encouraged risk-taking, and eventually became a habit. Fear faded, replaced by a desire for more adventures. We began exploring remote places at various phases of the night, venturing into small towns around Vikarabad, Sangareddy, Patancheru, almost touching the border of other states. Stories of dacoits and looters on some routes beyond Ananthagiri hills at night made us cautious, but it didn't stop us. We started sticking more to highways.

Have you ever spent a full night on a motorcycle?

It is an altogether different experience. You need to be very careful about where to stop for a break due to various risky reasons. Some bikers carry Chilli spray or a few safety items for emergencies. We used to carry risks. However, the highway was at least a safer place comparatively. Truckers and Dhabas made it relatively safer.

We stopped at our first break near Outer Ring Road (ORR), the last crowded place you'll see after leaving the city. I pulled a cigarette from a pack in my upper pocket, held it between my lips, took out a lighter, and covered the tip with my other hand. The smell of the gas and a deep blow. It was an amazing feeling. The night was getting colder. After a few drags, I passed it on to Ravi. Our tastes in music matched perfectly. We enjoyed philosophical talks, which went on for a long time, sometimes throughout our all-night rides. It gave a different high. We usually carried a few Heritage wine bottles, small enough to be kept in our jeans' pockets. Wine added depth to our discussions. It was not safe, but many things we do in life aren't.

We started after a 15-minute break, and as we rode for a few more miles, even truck traffic became lesser and lesser. We were riding at a slow pace ahead of Isnapur. Ravi took out our first bottle, and we started taking a few sips round by round. I was usually the driver, and

Ravi used to light the fire with some philosophical pointers or trigger a song, and then we used to go ahead with the flow together. There were small towns on the way where the service road had a cement walking path, and we used to sit beneath the streetlight for a smoke break. I loved that feeling. Freedom. When the whole town is in deep sleep and nobody is there to judge or bother you. It is your time.

After a brief break, we continued our ride and crossed Sangareddy. We were familiar with all the turns, potholes, and everything around. Probably in 15-20 mins, we were about to reach another town, Peddapur, and we saw something going on besides the highway on a service road. We were driving at a normal speed, around 50-60 kmph. I slowed down as we watched from a distance. A lady was shouting loudly while sitting behind a man on a bike. That was an unusual view for us at around 1:30 AM.

Probably a family argument. It must be in Telugu. Better to ignore and pass on. "But what if she needs help? "Ravi questioned. I now was not sure if it was Ravi or the wine inside him. As we came closer, we could hear both of them shouting loudly, and it gave me a kick as well. We talk about all the harassment, rapes, and how society needs to grow stronger to avoid them while sitting comfortably in the four walls watching TV.

But what would you do when you actually come across such situations? Ignore and pass on? We were confused, and they both were not aware of us passing by. Probably. What if that is a trap? The human mind thinks about all the critical things. It has immense power to safeguard us from risky situations. It is difficult to choose between this human mind or an emotional heart when you have very little time to think, and it is an odd time, and you have heard many stories in the past. And usually, you will find yourself in a decision-making situation when all these three things are together.

We were now quite close to them but were afraid to come to a standstill. It looked like she was falling behind from his parked bike. Many thoughts reiterated. Family matter, harassment, is he forcefully taking her, is there a medical condition, is she needing help, and thousands of things. We went a bit ahead and took a glance back. We could not control our emotions and went back slowly, staying on the highway. Ravi got down and went a few steps closer. I was ready with the bike in case it was needed. It was intense.

I saw that lady fell down from the bike and hurriedly parked mine and rushed towards the location. We were not able to understand what that man was saying but figured out that he is her husband, and she is in labor. Screaming out loud. I was witnessing something like this for the first time. It was unbearable pain for her. You can imagine she was not bothered about anything. It was difficult to stay calm hearing all her screams. We asked the man what happened. And he managed to tell us that he was going to get her to the hospital tomorrow but the pain started late at night unexpectedly. He was alone and poor. It felt so bad.

My mind started thinking about options now; Ola Uber is only for the city, and we don't know anyone around, not even the language.

I moved to the highway and started taking the last chance. I planned to stop the first vehicle I could see by waving and doing all the signals. Few cars passed by with no luck, and her screams were getting louder as hell. Ravi and I stood in the middle of the road now. She was laying down beside the road, and he was besides trying to calm her. Again, a few cars passed by dodging us. Finally, we were able to stop a car and saw a woman in the backseat. We felt a bit relieved for a reason. We thought a woman would be able to understand the situation and help us. We explained the situation to them. They were reluctant initially but then agreed. We requested the woman to help us lift her.

That woman in the car probably had hesitation lifting up an unknown village woman.

I so much felt at that moment that her husband should have talked a bit in Telugu to get the required help but probably he was also disturbed by the situation.

With no second thought, I called Ravi and lifted her. Carefully kept her in the back seat while she was screaming in pain. But probably she realized that there were people around and she was getting the help. I thought. Her husband seated with her in the back, and others managed seating in front. Ravi had taken out his bike keys and handed them over to him. We asked them to hurry towards the hospital And they left.

We watched the car go, and the scream got dimmer and dimmer. Thank god that car stopped by. We felt relieved. We went back towards the sidewalk. Sat down and lit a cigarette each. It felt lighter but heavier as well. We realized so many things in these past hours.

Not all are lucky to have a comfortable life. Some face the toughest of the situations we could hardly imagine.

We criticize others while watching such news from the comfort of our homes, but we are no different when in situations. We try to ignore and skip when we see a fight going on around, or a woman being harassed. We conveniently close our eyes and still call ourselves heroes in stories that we paint to our near and dear ones. If people become more and more empathetic and understand each other regardless of boundaries, we would no longer need such heroes.

We were hesitating to lift her in front of her husband initially, but realized that we should be least bothered about any misinterpretations or judgments if the help we offer is with our purest emotions.

We turned back for home. No words were uttered. No philosophies. Just the silence. And hopes for those two to reach safely to the hospital and get all the help they need.

_ Vikrant _

Punch the Clock

Simmi and her Friend (Sandy) were planning to have vacation. It's been year they have not been to any place together, they always discussed but never complete or executed the plans they had (As it happens with most of us). This time they both agreed and finalized destination which was Andaman & Nicobar(A&N)

It's an island of India and have to take flight to reach that place. They were excited to see the place, beautiful oceans, explore the history of place and was wondering around their own thoughts. Sandy was tripped in his own thoughts of laying around the beach , relaxing at resort pool , clearing his mind with doing nothing , on other hand Simmi was on top of world with all her imagination on how she is going to wonder around the street , explore each and every place, eat things she never ate and not going to miss the uniqueness of Andaman & Nicobar that it has beautiful sunset & sunrise everyday along the beach .

The day cane when they flew to A&N; reached in evening and all set to explore the place. Simmi told Sandy to be awake by 3am to watch Sunrise, Sandy was onboard (Half heartly) and thought not start her trip by spoiling it. They both woke up and headed towards sunrise and it was magnificent (Sandy was amazed to see that and thanked her silently). They relaxed all day along at resort at pool, had some drinks and headed towards sunset to another beach and their evening making beautiful memories. They arrived hotel late night and again Simmi said be ready to watch the sunrise at 3 am, Sandy said we saw it today and why we have to get up so early, we got whole day planned for us.

Simmi did not listen to him and said if you are not willing to go, i will go and wake you up once am back. He got furious and thought she is being selfish and not letting him enjoy as he wants (He forgot they spent whole day at resort around the pool as he wanted) and went to sleep with grumpy goodnight. She woke up next morning, woke him up but he denied going and she headed her way out for sunrise. She arranged vehicle with help of hotel staff, and it was planned to arrive in next 10min. By the time vehicle was there she saw Sandy coming out of the room with his grumpy face and big eyes which feels like planning to kill Simmi.

On the way to beach it started to drizzle and driver asked would you still want to move ahead, Simmy said yes, and Sandy could not stop himself and started arguing that why do you think it's still good to go as we won't be able to see the sunrise. Simmi kept quiet and let it sink to avoid the argument but that made Sandy more furious. After few min Simmi replied that i still want to see that beach and hoping drizzle will stop and she will be able to see the sunrise. She doesn't know if she is ever going to come back here or not and why to waste time sleeping which she can do when at home.

Sandy didn't know what to say and kept going towards the beach and what they saw was unbelievable. There were 100's of people gathered on that beach (which was not same previous day) and waiting to have the sunrise. When they enquired around and found that it was the only day in a year when sun looks way bigger than normal days during sunrise and feels like you are almost near to it.

They waited for half an hour and not sure if Simmi's wish came true or it was just her lucky day as Sun started showing up and became a memorable for everyone gathered around. By seeing that Sandy could not stop himself and hugged Simmi to say thanks and being so persistent on what she wants. Sandy couldn't wait for sunset of that day as he knew it's going to be awesome, and he was behind Simmi for not being late for this. Simmi was happy to see Sandy is enjoying nature and happily being part of it.

This way they enjoyed sunrise and sunset of next 3 days during the trip and took the most beautiful memories along with them.

It was time to go back home after their last beach visit at A&N. They reached beach but by that time they were no longer very curious to see the beach as it was afternoon with sun straight on their head and doesn't feel like fun and they thought to go back hotel early and get some rest. The moment they started moving back Simmi saw few people going behind the trees where arrow says 1km ahead. Being spontaneous and not willing to leave a place which she knew exist but didn't see, she got curious to know what's there. She asked sandy to follow the people and see what's there, Sandy was not in mood to walk for 1Km without knowing where it will lead them.

Simmi insisted multiple time, but he denied then Simmi said OKAY let me go and find it out and will see you here in sometime. Sandy knew that she is not going to stop and being a lovely friend, he followed her to that path. They walked through narrow walk streams, small wooden bridges, dense forest where they could hear waves sound against the stone beach but couldn't see them, they saw many new birds and some they could just hear. After walk of around half an hour they reach to a place which was on the edge and Tip of the mountain where it was so breezy that they couldn't stand straight and view was jaw dropping, they could see blue ocean all three sides of them as they were standing on the tip of the cliff. That was the best moment of their trip and they felt like they have found a treasure which was dug deep inside ground and not known to anyone.

While coming back from view they both were happy and thinking how crazy Simmi was to just walk through the road without knowing the destination and that made Sandy realized that Simmi does know how to create beautiful moment being in now without thinking of if's and buts and she was right that Time is now to explore not to sleep.

_ Usha _

Seat Number 15

After a week-long vacation, Sandip was boarding his train on a Saturday evening and the station was less crowded than usual. 16-hour journey to Kolkata which he used to do from his hometown. He entered his coach, placed his bag beneath his seat, plugged in his earphones and started scrolling his Spotify lists. Train started and he could notice only a few people in his compartment. It was probably after 10-15 mins that a girl came dragging her bags and started looking for her seat from the aisle.

"Mine is 15" She said pointing at the opposite seat. An old lady nodded and moved away from the window. Sandip gave a helping hand as she pushed in her bags and she got seated. He, "Where did you get in from?" It was a while since the train had left the station and had not stopped after that. "I was late and entered a random coach. Had to cross 4 wagons with all these bags." She replied. Sandip gave a smile and continued with his music and social networking routine. She took a while to settle and then took out a book to read.

Sandip, while listening to Luke Combs and Blake Shelton while peeping out of the window, was ensuring taking a glance at the girl on Seat number 15. She was beautiful. With an elegant traditional attire, she had a sober personality. She was reading Nicholas Sparks. Sandip tried to resist looking at her, at least trying to keep sufficient gaps in between but he wasn't able to.

He was a single man who started working in this city a couple of years ago. Just so that you know his history and experience in these things, He had faced rejections from a few girls in the past and had a short-term relationship which did not go well. He was thinking about an opportunity to talk with her but she was immersed in the book. At around 8 PM she closed her book, drank water and peeped outside the window. It was dark but still visible outside. In the next half an hour or so, their eyes might have met each other while Sandip was trying to check her out but ignored. He felt uncomfortable and wanted to get some distraction. He thought and walked in the passage between two coaches to take a break. Stations were passing by intermittently. He spent some time taking a fresh breeze and came back to his place. She was having her home-made sandwiches. Sandip took out his tiffin, had dinner and walked to the passage for hand washing.

Stood behind her for his turn. "Nicholas Sparks Fan?" He broke the ice. "Not really. Reading his book for the first time after watching The Notebook." He smiled. "Are you into reading?" She asked. "I was, I was. I started with Chetan Bhagat and then Paulo Coelho and then a few of Nicholas Sparks as I wanted more and more depth but nothing now." She gave a smile and went back to her seat. He stayed there for a while. Enjoying the moment. Remembering her smile. It is just a matter of train journey. Tomorrow morning, we will be on our separate ways. Still our mind looks for opportunities. In the middle of nowhere. Finding out possible within the impossible. He felt.

After a short break people prepared their bed. Bright lights no longer lit the aisle. Lights coming from the window still kept things visible. "So why did you stop reading?" He heard her voice and turned his face. Train was running at speed and lights were flashing intermittently on her face. "I thought of writing my own. Have started lately as a hobby." "Interesting. What do you write?", She said. "Till now I've been writing small poetries, but I want to publish a novel of my own one day", Sandip replied. "Wow! I would like to read your work". His heart ran at a much faster rate. But his brain ran a bit faster on how he can share. Should he ask for her number to message her his few best poetries? He thought for a while. "Do you have an insta page where I can check out?" She asked. Sandip's train of thoughts stopped at once.

Opportunity missed. "Yes. Sure.". He showed his Instagram account on the phone. "I will definitely check it out. Thanks" And she started checking her phone. After a while her phone rang and she got on a call. A Long call. "Is it her boyfriend?", Sandip wondered. He felt curious but could not make it out. He waited for an hour but could not see her. It was all dark in the compartment. Many thoughts floated around in his mind and he fell asleep.

He woke up in the morning at around 8 and she seemed to be still asleep. It was almost time to get off the train in the next 30 minutes when she woke up. "Should I ask her about her call last night? It would be too personal. She may not like it. How to talk to her. Will this story get over with the train journey?" Many thoughts wandered and went away but he could not dare to talk. They took out their bags as the station approached and hurried towards the exit. She was waiting on the platform, checking out her phone, probably trying to call someone and he left the station. Boarded a cab and went back home. But his mind was still on the journey. He thought of all the things he could have said.

He lived alone in an apartment and spent all Sunday thinking about the journey. It took him a few days to forget the incident and get back to routine. Mind introspects in many details after something interesting has happened. After a week's time he saw a unique like on his page from Tweety_Sweety. DP had an image of Nicholas Sparks Book and Sandip could immediately figure it out. He sent a friend request and again started waiting impatiently. In just a few minutes his request was accepted and he sent out a message to her, "I hope you read my page. Can we meet for feedback?". Later he thought if he looked desperate but the train had already left the station.

And then they meet. Probably it was destined that way. They had planned to meet for coffee and breakfast but they spent the whole day together. They met again the next weekend and began spending time together, exploring the city restaurants, malls, sharing their dreams and aspirations with each other and supporting each other in their missions. And after spending weekends for months and months Sandip proposed to her. He wanted to do it personally when they met but his emotions slipped off during a late-night call and he did it. She was surprised and straightaway rejected. She wanted to continue being good friends but he had gone much ahead in his thoughts. He disconnected the call and switched off his cell phone.

She was worrying that her parents may not agree to this idea of marrying a Bengali boy. She was from Kerala and there is a good cultural difference between them. But she also felt sad rejecting him. They both cried the whole night at their places.

A month of struggle passed by. They chatted with each other but it started with casual updates and ended with fights on the relationship. And then Sandip stopped talking to her. He understood that it needs patience and control to get things he wants. Things are not always straightforward. He started typing and just before he sent, he used to control himself. He knew she also might be missing him. Finally, after a couple of weeks she sent a message and they planned to meet.

She told all the reasons she is pushing him back and he convinced her that she will never be in trouble because of him. He made her comfortable and ensured that they would handle the situation together. She understood and agreed and again went back to square one after a week. It took a good time for her to be comfortable and then one fine day she agreed. Sandip felt like a winner that day. But it was a short-lived moment.

She told about this to her family and they got angry and were not at all willing to understand the situation. She was so close to her family that she wanted them to be happy. She told this to Sandip and he wanted to go with her and convince her parents. But she did not like this idea. Again, a few months of struggle passed by. Finally, Sandip had to ask her if she would be happy with him or should they get separated. She left that too unanswered.

Sandip's family on the other hand was putting pressure. They were open and had no issues with him marrying Sneha but if she was not ready, they were asking to marry a girl of their choice. When Sandip was about to leave for his hometown to meet a girl their family had identified, she called him. Shouted on him because she loved him and wanted him to take her responsibility now. His heart melted again. It's a difficult phase as always.

Later he took her to her hometown and met her family. They were not agreeing but seeing his dedication, humbleness and love towards her they got convinced that they will think about this. A month later after they returned to Kolkata, she said that her family was ready and wanted to meet his family. They all met and liked each other and then got married. Later they gave birth to a cute Son.

When they look back now, they always remember their first train journey together and their weekend outings. They remember the night of the proposal. They remember the fights. They remember their journey to her hometown. They remember all the struggle.

Today when their 8-year son was asking Sandip, "Dad what is love exactly?" Sneha remembered this whole journey as she was listening to his answer while in the kitchen.

"Love is all the struggle and pain we go through for achieving something we dream of".

"What after we achieve it dad?"

"Then it becomes your life my son", Sandip replied.

_ Vikrant _

Stoppage

It's been 2 and half years me and my wife got married. We often think about our future which involves carrier, travel, retirement and family which also includes having kids.

When we met before marriage which was neither arrange or love, we met over matrimonial sites and we discussed everything which felt important to us at that point of time (where will settle, what kind of life style we enjoy, how will manage finance, family and many things) but there was one discussion which I remember vividly and that was about having kids.

It was our second meet in person; she had flown from Bangalore to meet me in Pune. We were really excited to meet each-other as we have been talking over phone and video call from last month and everything was really going very well. My mind was not thinking questions but all scenarios or possibilities of what could happen when we meet. The day came when she arrived in Pune and came to meet me, we had great time together and it was about time to leave, and we were standing outside of my building waiting my roommate to bring my dog downstairs for a walk. He came and she met him with kisses, and all love she had to pour, and he was enjoying it the most (My dog not my friend) and then we continued for walk. At that point she asked me about what i think about kids in life, she clarified herself that she doesn't want to have one but totally happy to adopt one. I always loved kids but was not very mandate to have one , i was also okay to adopt one and when i said that , i could see relief in her eyes and face hut she stated that she might feel different later and may want to have kids and i told her that its totally up to you as you are the one who has to carry the baby for 9months and it should be your choice .She didn't say anything then but after marriage she told that she was impressed by my answer and i think that's where she locked me as her groom (Thank god i was talking sense that day).

We got married and everything worked out the way it was thought of, and things started falling in place; it made us so happy we started excelling in their career as well. We are supporter of one another, pushing each other to excel and do our best and came together as Lego pieces. Same time our families kept pushing us for having kids and increase the family but both of us knew what they had decided and kept the same page ongoing.

Now here we are after 2and half year talking on same things and kids are in the picture but with same answer. It was Sunday afternoon we both were talking on general day today thing and we came to last question as "Are we ready to have kids in life". Both of us didn't have any straight answer and we started stating things like

We do not understand each other communication well.

We both are looking to get promoted in our carrier.

We still fight on silly things which sometimes doesn't even matter to is next day.

We haven't bought house for us or made any-any-another property/asset.

We are learning to deal with our parents amicably.

This list kept growing and we spent almost half an hour on this and later on the conclusion of our discussion was "we are not ready" and we made plans to comeback on this topic after 6months.

We kept enjoying their life with fun and adventure in life. One fine day she was planning to have short trip on weekend ahead of my birthday (his birthday was on weekdays) and surprise me with this trip plan. Couple of days before the planned weekend her boss called her and said that he is putting her through promotion cycle, and she should be ready for interview.

She was surprised, excited, happy and on cloud nine by hearing the good news and she shared it with husband and he was extremely happy for her. We continued with our trip with double happiness and opportunity ahead.

Interview date came and it was coinciding with my birthday but as we have already been to trip and knowing this is a big opportunity, we agreed to same date and supporting each other through this time. I am sure she felt so happy that she has chosen a right partner for her, who is with her every time and supporting her in each step of her life (She never told me, but I know she thinks that way). Interview went through and she got promoted.

She was full of energy and wanted to do more as she got what she has worked for and always wanted this as next steps. It felt like nothing can go wrong and universe is with us only. The day her promotion got effective, she felt like chasing more and going above and beyond. For a week at least she woke up with smile on her face and truly in peace.

After couple of days, she came to me and said she has missed her monthly cycle, but we were relaxed and thought it might be late but let's just have pregnancy test to be confirm. We carried out first test and it came "positive", and we were shocked to see those two pink lines and searched through google to know if it could be wrong and we found that it could be wrong due to multiple factors, so we got second kit and that gave the same result.

We both had no idea what to do, how to react, whom to ask, should we feel happy or sad; it was just silence in the room.

We decided to go to doctor next day to remove this confusion.

She felt like her world got unmeasurable turbulence and everything came in front of eyes, the interview, promotion, new journey, dreams and the decision they took before getting married.

Next day at hospital we went to doctor and informed what we found on test and asked her to carry some test which can remove this doubt. She was smiling as she could read what we were going through and politely continued for test and after 5mins we were able to hear the heartbeat of our kid. This was not the confirmation but the validation that it happened. We still had no idea how to react and we came home by saying will think and let her know our decision. It was a quiet ride to home at outside but mind was blowing with thoughts, questions, stupid ideas and more importantly what she is thinking, why she is not saying anything, what does she want, what am supposed to do in this scenario, what if she doesn't want the baby or what if she wants. I did not realize when we reached home, we entered inside and sat on the same table where 1 week ago we concluded that we are not ready for this.

She felt like she was on top of world and not sure where this new information will take her. She had habit of introspecting herself continuously. so, she asked her husband not to tell the family and lets just sink this information and think calmly in couple of days as we have time in case, we need to do any action. Her husband agreed and supported her as always by saying that whatever your decision would be am with you as you are the one who is important to me, and you know what's best for you.

They both again supported each other with this decision and went silent on it. She sat alone for couple of days introspecting the situation, remembering everything happened in couple of weeks and she could see herself happy through all this because of the achievement she has accomplished and thoughts that crossed her mind.

At that moment she noticed one thing. multiple thoughts crossed her mind but except one and the thought was "not to have this baby "or "get rid of it "or "it will ruin her life" whole thoughts were around how it will impact the life but not how to get away from it. This made her realize that she is not the same she was before marriage and her thinking have changed unconsciously and maybe she is not ready to go through this but same time her inner self is not opposing it.

She discussed it with her husband, and he again asked her to think for couple of days in case she might have been emotional during this decision making. She agreed and went on with her daily routine but thought of missing out things when she will not be around in office or people going ahead of her in her absence and she might not get next promotion soon make her anxious every other moment.

She had to get all of this out of her mind, and she thought to connect with her mentor, and she was surprised that still thought of leaving the baby never cross by. The day she was supposed to meet her mentor, she was driving in good speed and ahead of others as she is passionate about driving but had to stop for signal and rest of cars also came and stood beside or just behind her. Later when it was green signal and time to go, she saw couple of cars moved ahead of her as they got passage fast or they had better cars but after few mins she was driving parallel to them and had left some behind. It made her think of her pregnancy situation that this is just a small stoppage in her journey but if she comes back with same drive and passion to work, she will be able to take charge over career. Their might me still few who has gone ahead or was behind and came beside but it doesn't mean she will fall behind. This cleared all the thoughts or confusion in her mind and made her smile by thinking that this is going to be a great stoppage in her life which is going to come with great learning and beautiful memories of life.

_ Usha _

A Deeper Dream

Did this ever happen to you? You woke up from a beautiful dream and for a fraction of seconds after opening your eyes you are in a doubt. Doubt about which side of it is true. That beautiful dream or the reality.

I had a similar experience just now. But it was a lot deeper than you can imagine.

I woke up today with great excitement. It was a day I was waiting for since long. Since childhood I was into art, mostly spiritual paintings.

I remember my first sketch of Shiva I did when I was 12. Since then, it has been a long journey. I own numerous awards and recognition for my work. But that is not what motivates me. I enjoy reading religious stories and scriptures. And when I read them, I get involved in them. I get so deeply involved that I become one of those characters in the story and start living it. I enjoy the bliss and beauty of those moments. And then when I hold my paint brush gently and look at the canvas it is not at all blank. I see all the setup already there. I just start spreading colours and blending them till I find it done. It is not the outcome that fascinates a true artist. But the process. Each time I start a new one, it makes me enjoy and experience the moments I could never get a chance to live.

I woke up with excitement this morning just because I was going to start working on a new plan today. I had gathered all the articles I needed. Queued up the music I liked in my playlist. Everything was properly set up. But as I started reading, I felt a pain in my chest. And this gradually increased. It was like my chest was squeezing itself from inside. And I found it difficult to breathe. I fell down on my back. It did not hurt much. I was thinking whether I could get up and call the doctor and decided to muster up all my energy. I made an attempt to crawl but in vain. I fell down again and now I lost my will. I just laid down waiting for whatever happened next to happen. The squeezing kept on increasing and now I could barely breathe. I was still conscious.

Soon as I realized something serious was happening thoughts started rushing into my mind. My childhood. Friends and family. And I remembered the time I left all of them and came to this city. Just to pursue my hobby. All came like a flash. Time slowed down for a while. I remembered the efforts I had put in to become successful. I remembered how people praised me for all my paintings. They used to say that moments captured in those paintings connected them more and more with the Almighty God. The facial expressions in those paintings seemed realistic to them. And how with every painting I became more mature.

I thought I was nearing death. I could not breathe anymore. But still, I could think. I never imagined it would work like this. I could not feel my body parts but just could see the ceiling fan still working. I could hear very dimly the music I had played. Thoughts started popping up in my head. Will I be going into Heaven or Hell?

After a while, all the listening went off as well as the vision. Time still was moving with slower speed. Nothing inside my body is alive except my brain. It still is doing its job and I could think and feel. Till this point, you could try hard and imagine the phases I experienced.

But as soon as my brain stopped working, all my thinking stopped and the only thing I could still do is feel. This is quite impossible for you to imagine. We have never known or read about the possibility of this happening. But believe me. I could feel it. After brain death, the time started speeding up.

I had no relation to my physical body anymore. I had seen in movies that spirits have a body but could not be seen. I realized that all is a false imagination. They also show in movies that spirits could see and listen but then why was there a need of putting ears and eyes into our physical bodies. I understood that people imagine and show only what they can, with their limited brain capacity.

I was waiting for God to come. Now, not for showing me the path to heaven or hell. Not to tell me some words of wisdom. Just to come and make me feel that he exists. I had spent all my life trying to make people believe in him. To explain to people that he exists. And all my fame and success were because I was able to help people connect with him. But there was no evidence of him I could feel. It felt bad.

I felt like going back to my room to see my paintings, to touch them and think about how I felt the presence of God if he does not exist at all. Habits make you think about even those things which you can no longer do. But eventually I realized about the loss of my abilities to do any of those things.

This was the time when formless me started living into the feelings completely. The only thing I had of my own. It felt relaxing. There were no expectations, no dreams, no desires, no pressures, no schedules, no task lists, no actions and reactions, no consequences, no convincing, no religion, no racism, no borders, no laws, no rules, no comparison, no struggle and absolutely nothing. Only a formless self. It felt like life. It felt much more than living. It felt perfect. It felt like God. And it felt like it was with me throughout my life, unknowingly.

I had thought about many different concepts of God while working on my paintings. That is what usually people do. Everyone on earth has his own different concept of God which he keeps following. Everyone on earth tries to prove the might of his God. Everyone tries to influence others. But today only after I left my body and everything I had; I realized the mistake I made throughout my life.

I tried to believe in God, I did whatever it takes to do that. I read stories, made paintings, and played music. I tried doing everything to connect with God. The only thing I never did was to live the God I had inside.

Beep .... Beep .... Beep ....

Somewhere between these thoughts, my alarm clock woke me up. It suddenly felt like the whole life I lived was like a dream. It was temporary.

Did this ever happen to you? You woke up from a beautiful dream and for a fraction of seconds after opening your eyes you are in a doubt. Doubt about which side of it is true. That beautiful dream or the reality. I had a similar experience just now. But it was a lot deeper than you can imagine.

_ Vikrant _

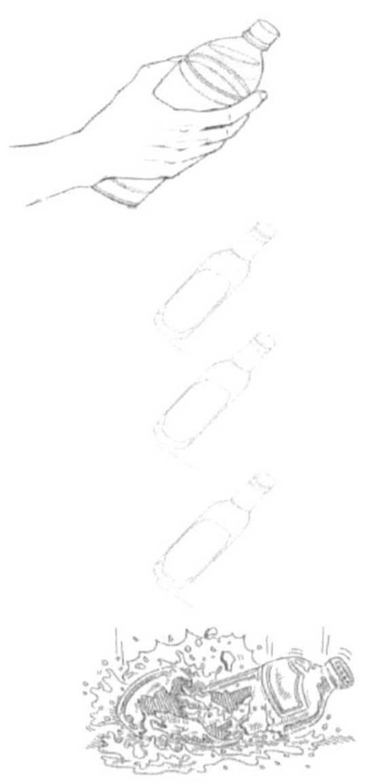

Hold It Tight

Those days when it's been 4/5 years out of college and you have started getting into money, relationships, friends, family, savings, enjoying in moment but haven't understood anything completely.

Every small knowledgeable word or phrase looks an eye opener, wisdom falling in lap.

One guy named Andy was working in IT firm from last 4 years and in those 4 years he had tried to live his life on his own condition without thinking about future, roamed around, went out with friends, had vacations and felt free. One weekend they were having fun all together and after couple of hours everyone was feeling relaxed talking to each other and suddenly glass slipped from one of friend's hand and splits into multiple small pieces and he shouted, oh my God that was my favourite glass and I had always kept it with love and attention.

Then another friend said if it was that worthful and loved, why you didn't hold it with full grip and should have taken special care of it; what's the use of crying now. This sentence suddenly made Andy realized something and started reminded him of that incident when he was planning to go on solo trip with couple of unknown people and plan was to travel to 3-4 places.

He was excited as always to capture the moments, enjoy the sceneries, spend his day well, feel the money he had earned up and fulfil all dreams he had during childhood. Next day he got call from his dad and regular chit chat on how day is going and what next. He told his father that he is planning this trip and he will have fun and will share pictures.

His father told him if you have time come home, visit us, we are missing your presence. Will have fun together and plan something here.

He said he will think and let his father know but he didn't think much about it and planned his trip further. One day before leaving for trip he informed his father that he is going for trip and next time he will visit home.

He moved ahead with plan and reached destination and did video call to his father and family to show them the scenic view and they were really happy that he is enjoying but still thinking it would have been great if he were with them. It was 5th day when he got call from one of his childhood friends and he started blabbering multiple things and Andy couldn't understand anything.

His friend said just come home and your father is not feeling well, and he couldn't understand what, why and how but he searched on how he can go back but there was no transport available until tomorrow morning.

He informed his friend and family that he will start tomorrow and reach home day after. He couldn't sleep whole night thinking all bad possibilities his family might go through. He kept every min update from his frond and gave all financial support needed but he couldn't let go of thought that his father asked to come and meet them and if he would have chosen that as priority, he would have been with them and wouldn't have felt helpless at this point.

This made him think about all previous incident on how he has kept himself as priority all the time without realizing what next person is looking for and he remembered specifically that he had same in his relationship and thought she is not able to understand what he seeks but actually he didn't realize that he never kept her even equal forget about priority.

Next day he left towards home and found everything is fine and found that father was unconscious for longer time but nothing to worry about.

He hugged his father family tightly and thanks god that everything is fine, and his family didn't have to go through tough time.

His friends started asking him what happened, why he seems so lost and upset and he said I was thinking on how I should hold things tight before I lose my grip and feel regretful later.

_ Usha _

Anvi - My Love

It was the 23rd of September 2021, a Thursday that remains etched in my memory. How could I ever forget that day?

Thursdays were typically packed with meetings for me, but on this particular day, I was determined to reach home early. It was Anvi's 6th birthday – Anvi, my daughter, my love. She had a simple request, a Barbie-designed sling bag. While my wife was busy preparing the cake and Anvi's favourite dishes, the only ask from both of them was for me to be home by 8 PM, which meant leaving Hitech City no later than 7:30 PM. I had meticulously planned my work week, focusing on preparing for the progress review meeting scheduled for the evening. However, my plans took an unexpected turn when my boss called me into his office.

Walking in with a half-made slide deck, I anticipated a discussion about the progress meeting. To my surprise, I received news that shook me to the core – I had lost my job. Like many who faced similar situations during the Covid era, I found myself among the unemployed.

Struggling to comprehend the situation, I started driving aimlessly, contemplating the various reasons behind this sudden turn of events. Thoughts flooded my mind – about my family, their needs, liabilities, and societal expectations. Finding a quiet spot at the beginning of the Outer Ring Road (ORR), I parked my car safely, leaned against the wall, and tried to process how my life had taken a sudden U-turn. It was 3 PM, and the events of the day weighed heavily on my mind. As I contemplated the next steps, darker thoughts crossed my mind, but the faces of my wife and daughter prevented me from taking any drastic measures. Aware that job opportunities were scarce in the current economic climate, I grappled with the uncertainty of my future.

By 4 PM, hunger had eluded me, and I found myself inundated with messages and calls from my wife. Unable to face her or check the messages, I contemplated various excuses to avoid going home.

Exhausted and on the verge of giving up, I mustered the strength to drive back home.

Anvi greeted me enthusiastically upon opening the door, unaware of the turmoil within me. Despite my internal struggles, I went through the motions of interacting with my family. As I entered the bedroom to change, I suddenly collapsed, unconscious.

My wife, with the help of our neighbours, rushed me to a nearby hospital, ensuring Anvi was cared for in my absence. That night, my wife stayed by my side in the hospital. In the midst of physical pain, I mustered the courage to share the news of losing my job. She paused, then tears streamed down her face.

"You fell down at home. What if it had happened while you were driving or outside? We cannot fathom our lives without you. We can adjust to a simpler life, endure basic necessities, and I can work to support you. We can manage with less, but losing you is something we cannot afford. Anvi didn't hesitate to stay back at the neighbours when I asked her to. She was deeply worried about you." She controlled her emotions, realizing our current situation.

After a brief moment, she went to wash her face, returning with newfound strength. From that day on, I witnessed the resilience of one of the strongest women on earth. Anvi hugged me the next day, not questioning about her birthday but expressing her concern through a warm, comforting embrace.

After an extensive job hunt and support from friends, I secured another job with similar remuneration after a month and a half. Anvi and my wife stood by me during this challenging period.

Today is the 23rd of September 2022. The day I will never forget for two reasons. Anvi's birthday and the day that made me realize that failures are temporary. With a resilient spirit, one can overcome temporary setbacks. It underscored the importance of life – jobs may come and go, but life is irreplaceable. Moreover, it emphasized the significance of family.

This experience also taught me the importance of preparedness for life's surprises and failures. Life may not provide a notice before throwing challenges our way, making it essential to prepare for the worst while savouring the best moments.

_ Vikrant _

Assumed Horizons

It's around 5 in evening and sun is setting down while making whole sky orange and slowly converting into pinkish. Vinay is sipping tea in balcony while enjoying the sunset and thinking that he should also have such vibrant energy which goes from morning till night without dropping for even minute.

His mother comes with an envelope which is delivered at their doorstep with Vinay name on it. Vinay checked from where it is, and it was from college she had applied.

He was excited to open it up as he was planning to be in this college from last year, but he wanted to open it up with his best friend to share the news.

He called his friend Vaibhav and asked her to come over, he lives just 5min away from Vinay. They both are friends since childhood because of friendship between their friends. They both went to same school since crash classes, studied piano, Guitar and played all sports together. They were like two sides of a coin which were difficult to apart.

Vaibhav came quickly leaving everything behind as he knew how much it matters to Vinay. He entered in house and ask Vinay's mother to order some sweets and snacks for the bigger news and mother was completely clueless what Vaibhav was talking about. Vinay shouted from balcony "Aye Stupid, stop finding reason to eat, just tell her you want something to eat, and she will give it to you" then his mother started laughing thinking that Vaibhav is just joking around.

Vaibhav came to balcony and asked Vinay, haven't you informed her yet? When are you going to tell her, while boarding flight? Are you insane to hide such thing from her? Tell me, does uncle knows about? Vaibhav had many questions as they had discussed about this earlier and Vinay was supposed to inform everything to his parents about applying for all colleges and he did inform them expect this college as it was in another city and wasn't sure how they are going to react.

Vaibhav got settled and Vinay's mother sent them quick snacks to munch with gossips. Vaibhav took sip of lemon iced tea and suddenly felt calmness within, it's one of his favourites beverages and he has been having it here since childhood. Vinay shook him up to come back to reality "Can you pls concentrate on situation more than your drink". Vaibhav jokingly says, "Your situation won't be as interested as this".

Vaibhav said, first of all tell me whether you got it college or not and then will see what to do next. Vinay gave the envelop to him and said i wanted to open it with you and Vaibhav jumped on it directly. Before Vaibhav could open it up, Vinay says do you think i am ready for this? I am not sure if am ready for it or not.

You have been waiting for this so long and now you think you are not ready? Why you think so? Vaibhav says he never had this feeling of doubt or uncertainty, it was always yes to everything and then Vaibhav says may be its because of your parents? You might be thinking about them more than you needed. Vinay was not convinced with it and says he needs time to think before he opens the letter. In both scenarios (Yes/No) he wanted to be prepared and not overthink later.

As his mother called them for dinner, they did not realize how long they have been talking (Which was not the first time). Vaibhav said he will go back home to have dinner and discuss on his college choices with them *(Hinting indirectly at Vinay).*

Vinay's family sat for dinner and his mother brought topic of college selection and listening to that his domestic helps say, "Bhaiya college jayenge" and started talking about her time when she wanted to go to college but didn't speak to her family thinking they won't agree or understand, which she regrets till today.

Vinay realizes that if he doesn't speak today, he might regret not sharing later and he started talking about his college selection and spoke about the college far from home in another city, but he is not sure he is ready or not to go far and be his own.

His parents told him that in life it's not always necessary that you are ready. Sometimes you just go with what you like, and it might take you far and in case if doesn't go that way you still learn a lot and you will not realize it today but later.

Which made lot of sense and he ask his domestic help to open letter for him and see what's inside.

She felt so happy that he is thinking so much about her and opened the envelope, and she speaks.

"Congratulations Vinay"

You have been selected …

Before she could read further, Vinay got up and shouted "Yes"" Yes" am selected.

Seeing Vinay in such happiness his parents knew that he really wanted to be in this college and Vinay realized that maybe he was afraid of seeing rejection in letter more than not being ready go far from that's why he was hesitant to open the letter.

His parents congratulated him, and they all had very fulfilling dinner with this good news. After dinner he calls Vaibhav and said, "Bhai shopping karni hai badi sari college ki" and Vaibhav understood that he discussed with family, and all is sorted and teased him that Vinay did not wait for him to open up the envelope. They both spoke for a while and enjoyed.

Vinay slept happily with dreams of going to college, having fun with roommate's and college canteen

_ Usha _

The Dad Dairies

As I drove my car through the busy streets, the sounds of the day's chaos still clustered in my mind. The everyday route now seems like an endless maze, each turn and intersection prolonging the journey back to the comfort of my home. The setting sun paints the sky, casting long shadows that mirror the weight that has settled upon my shoulders.

The honking of impatient drivers and the continuous hum of the city traffic serve as a constant reminder of the fast-paced world I am trying to leave behind. My fingers grip the steering wheel tightly, as if trying to anchor myself amidst the emotional whirlwind that swirls within. Frustration and fatigue intermingle, creating a heavy cloud that lingers around me, refusing to dissipate.

Between the noise and the movement, a ray of hope flickers within me, fuelled by the thought of my family that awaits me at home. The image of my 1-year-old Son and my Wife. The warmth of their presence serves as a beacon guiding me through the disarray of my thoughts. With each passing landmark, the weight of the day begins to lift, replaced by a growing anticipation of the comfort and solace that only home can provide.

As I step into the home, my one-year-old son's laughter fills the air, instantly lifting my mood. Playing with him, the weight of the day begins to fade, replaced by the joy of simple moments shared with loved ones. Conversations with my wife offer peace, reminding me that I am not alone in my struggles.

Following a satisfying lunch, I gently swing my little one with some soothing songs, hoping to lull him into a peaceful slumber. However, despite my best efforts, his eyes remain stubbornly open, his tiny limbs squirming with restless energy. With each passing minute, a sense of frustration begins to grow at my patience.

It is then that I learned from my wife that our baby had been napping extensively during the day under the care of the nanny. The realization leads to a bit more anger. A mixture of understanding and a bit of disappointment. I come to terms with the fact that the daytime playfulness with the nanny may have saved the established pattern of sleep at our homes, which now leads to this current struggle.

Somehow, I could put him to sleep thinking of another busy tomorrow at around 1 AM. He kept stirring and waking up repeatedly, his restless sleep mirroring my thoughts of the next day at work.

Somewhere in the mind of my 1-year-old Son a possibility -

As the night settled in, and my dad took me in his arms, I found myself wide awake, my little eyes twinkling with the expectation of playtime between me and my dad. I had made sure to catch up on my daytime naps, saving my energy for these special moments with my mom and dad. Despite my dad's gentle swinging and soothing whispers, the excitement within me refused to let the drowsiness take over. I kept moving in his arms, eager to be a part of the joy and laughter that I knew was just around the corner. My daytime nap had been a deliberate strategy and my way of preparing for the nighttime adventures and bonding that I cherished with my family.

_ Vikrant _

Love the way they Need!

A guy named Sid was living in Pune and working in finance dept. in one of MNC. He was staying with his friends (6) in shared apartments. They used to have lot of fun and weekends were the best part of their life. One day he bought a puppy Labrador home and named him "Google".

Google became loved one of every one and no one could resist without giving food or snacks after looking into those cute eyes. Google became like a member of this bigger family, he made everyone go for a walk-in morning, evening and sometime late night. This routine, love, fun continued for years.

When google was 7years old, Sid started searching a bride for him over couple of matrimonial portals like shadi.com, jeevansathi.com. He was facing a challenge of finding a girl who would agree to have dog in her life and love him as Sid does. Google was his lifeline, and he couldn't imagine having life without google. Keeping Google with him was more important than having a wife /partner who doesn't like Google.

One day he came across a girl and Sid had face multiple number of challenges /declines that he chose to start with conditions and if that works well then move ahead.

Sid started conversation saying that i have a dog and I won't leave him, and he was surprised to see the answer coming from another side. she replied that she had 2 dogs when she was kid and wanted to bring new one in life but couldn't be due to family restrictions. That was the moment where it started and after 6 months they were happily married.

When Google started living with both of them and in couple of days, she became first love of Google's life. He was always with her, roaming around, plying games, asking for food, barking to get attention and she also loved him unconditionally. As newlywed couple Sid and his wife use to have arguments as individual personality and not able to understand how to resolve their issues.

She diverted her time towards google and started spending time with Google and slowly she understood what Google is looking for, he wants people to tub his belly, rub his ears, talk with him in sweet voice, take him out for play, take him out for multiple walks, give him toys and she did all of that what he felt as love. In couple of months Google started loving her more than Sid, became very protective of her even if Sid cannot play with her. She got attached to Google more than Sid as their arguments were not decreasing anytime.

If Sid and his wife call Google at same time, Google will go to his wife not to Sid. It almost felt like he has disowned Sid and became Mumma's boy.

One day Sid and his wife were discussing the changes Google is showing, Sid was saying that he has become more expressing and happier from early, and they were laughing like Google might have found purpose of his life in her.

She was discussing what and all she keeps doing with him like playing, rubbing his belly etc. and that moment she realized that she is doing all what he wants and she is loving him the way he sees love and it clicked her that everyone sees love in different way and we should love others the ways they want not the way we see the love.

She implemented this in her, and Sid relationship and their arguments decreased significantly, and relation started becoming strong day by day.

_ Usha _

Sweet Sixteen

I was in my 16s, and after the exams, I had planned to visit my grandma for a few days. It was a small old town, with mountain ranges on one side and the sea on the other. A beautiful town with mango trees, sloping roofs, houses made of mud, and a population of around 10-15 thousand. I was waiting for these vacations to enjoy a change after a yearlong of focused studies.

I boarded a bus Saturday night, and early in the morning, I was there. It was a familiar place and I could walk down home. I moved the wooden door open, and that creaking sound was good enough for my granny, and she came up. I had my morning breakfast and went out for a walk in the mangroves. There was a small hut, and I could see a woman cooking something and a child beside her from the half-open door. I continued my walk, and it felt so pleasant.

The place gets hot and humid during the day, but in the morning hours and later in the night, it is comfortable. I came back after walking and saw the lady talking to my Granny. They recently rented this small home, as I understood later.

Family of three. Her husband abandoned her, and she left the family with her two young kids. She took work as a maid, helping people in cooking and cleaning for a few families. That keeps her busy for a few hours in the morning and evening. I had seen one of her kids during my morning walk, helping her in the household. After she left, I inquired with my granny about how she found this place and other random queries I had in mind.

After spending the day at home, I took a stroll in town and came back. Had dinner and was wondering how to spend the rest of the time. I came outside on the porch. I liked sitting on the swing here because of the ambiance. It gets darker and darker outside, and a dim yellow light hangs on the side wall. It feels pleasant all around.

In the dark, I saw a girl walking with a tiffin box. I guessed she was the neighbour Aunt's elder daughter, as no one came from outside the fence. She knocked on the door, went inside, and came back after a while. She was simple, shy, and didn't bother even looking at me and walked away.

The next day, I met her as she was helping her younger brother get ready for school, and her mother introduced me to the two. Abha and Aditya. Abha was 13, and Adi 9. She asked me where I lived and about my school. I went back and asked my Granny what happened to the family who lived there earlier. They had 2 kids of my age, and we used to play all day. I was expecting them. My granny told me that they got transferred to a nearby city for work.

As I woke up from a short nap around 4 pm, I saw Granny requesting Abha to get some stuff from the market. She suggested that I accompany her. She probably knew that I needed company to stay back for a few more days. It probably was true.

Abha came back after a while, and we started walking. Not sure what to talk to each other about. But I broke the ice. I asked her about her school. She sadly replied that they don't have money for educating both of them, so she has to sacrifice, and she also has to support her mom at home. But she likes reading her brother's books. I felt sad. We talked about our hobbies, interests, and I found the difference. How many expectations I had from my parents and how understanding and mature she is. We walked inside a vegetable mart. She started picking up vegetables, carefully inspecting them and putting them in a basket.

She weighed them, confirmed the amount, and took the change back after payment. We started walking to the other store where she bought some more daily stuff, and we started walking back. I asked her if she could join again after dinner to spend some time talking. She said she usually has to help her Mom In the household post dinner. Her mom gets tired after a day-long work. I said, "I understand".

I spent some time talking with my Granny about my routine at home and my next plans and then thought of laying down early. After a while, I heard a knock and went to the door. It was Abha.

Me: Hey WhatsApp! Are you looking for Granny?

Abha: Not right now, I thought of coming to you. Are you busy? I can go back.

I asked her to wait, and then we walked to the porch. We sat on the steps outside.

Abha: I felt bad while I said no to you to come back after lunch. I kept thinking about it and had to tell my mom about it after all the work was done. She allowed me for some time.

We talked about my routine in the city and hers in this town. I told her about my mom and dad.

Abha: My dad is a very angry man, and all my childhood is gone seeing my parents' fight. I think my mom is much better and happier here.

Me: Do you miss your dad?

Abha: The memories I have don't make me miss him so much. But when I hear stories like you and see other families, I do feel sad.

It touched me. I could imagine her pain. We kept on talking for an hour, and then she left.

I went back to sleep, but I had her in my thoughts all night. Her situation, her feelings, her pain. I so wanted to help her, but what a 16-year-old boy could do. Rather what anyone else can do when life puts you in a situation. One needs to accept it and deal with it.

The next few days went with the same routine. Conversations with Granny, Sleep, small walks in the backyard or in town, and sometimes talking with Abha. She used to visit during the day or at least for a few minutes after dinner. 2 more days left for me to return back home. My tickets were booked for Saturday. I was not expecting this, but I saw Abha's face turning sad when I told her about my return.

Friday Evening. Abha came earlier than usual.

Me: What happened? Are you not helping your mom today?

Abha: I lied to my mom today. For the first time. I told her that I am having a headache.

Me: What? She believed it? And still, she let you come here?

Abha: I told her Granny wanted some help and I will come back soon. I really wanted to meet you.

Me: Hey Abha, I am here tomorrow as well. Your mom will not like this. Granny will feel bad.

Abha: Let it be. You want me to go?

Me: No. Please wait. Let's face it tomorrow.

Abha: Can't you stay back for a few more days? I enjoy talking to you. I will again be alone once you are gone.

Me: I will have to go. My tickets are done. Abha: Will you remember me once you go back? Will you come again someday?

Me: I definitely will keep coming here. Thanks for spending time with me here and making my vacation wonderful. You are a good girl. I really appreciate the way you help your mom and my granny. I feel proud of you.

Her face was turning deem. I felt she was not listening carefully. I stopped for a while and looked to check if someone was around. There was no one. She seemed to not care about surroundings much. We heard her mom's voice from a distance. She probably was calling her home.

Abha: I wanted to tell you something. Not sure how to.

Her mom came towards the door. Abha probably heard the footsteps and brought her face back to normal.

Mom: It is so late. Time to sleep for both of you. Come Abha.

She left. I went back to sleep with her thoughts in mind. What was it that she wanted to tell me? Are there feelings for me which she wanted to express? Or it was just that she was feeling sad about me going that she wanted to tell me?

Saturday again was routine. But I kept waiting for her to come and meet me. But she did not till the evening. I tried walking in front of her home to take a chance, but her door was closed since afternoon. My bag was packed, and I was about to leave. I was so wanting to meet her. But I was also afraid. Not sure why, but I was.

I picked up my bag, took blessings from my Granny, and started walking. Opened the wooden door on the fence. I could not gather the strength to look back at her door. I felt probably the door was open, and she was watching me go. I was crying from inside, and probably she was having tears over her face. I kept on walking, but my heart wanted me to go back and knock on her door. Not always we can do what we want to. I boarded the bus, and as the journey started, I kept on missing her. She was simple, beautiful, and pure. Her ponytail hair. Small red bindi on her forehead. Simple way of dressing. But so warm at heart.

I am 30 now. But whenever I visit my Granny's place I still remember that week. I remember her. I remember that Friday night when she was about to share something with me. That shy girl whom I could never meet again.

They had left the place the next time I visited. That small hut was falling apart and remained vacant. But it was filled with the memories I had from my 16s.

_ Vikrant _

The Lost Touch

It's a lovely day, sun is bright and reflection of neighbour's window crossing through smalls plants and entering to house. Which makes the house a little shiny and reminds of sparkly shine coming through trees in forest.

Sound comes from door; comes fast we are getting late, and Disha replies, Yes coming! She tries to catch last moment things like her mobile, clutch, gives a check for lipstick and keep it in purse, her earring whether matching with dress or not, her hair tie in case she needs it later, wipes, sanitizer and last but not least Bindi on her head. Before stepping outside of rooms, she gives one last look to see if something is missing and she realizes that her room looks messy, and she have to clean once she is back and suddenly realizing that window is open. She quickly walks toward window and while closing it she notices a pink colour flower in neighbour's balcony which brings smile to her face.

Her husband (Kunal) looks at her and says one day i am going to be late and make you wait for me; she gives him a hug and says, Sure! He gets more frustrated as he knows she is saying it sarcastically and that day might not come. It was drive of 30mins to meet their friends and it was the road where most of flower nurseries are near the road. Disha loves this road as she can look for so many plants, flowers and greenery around which makes her happy and smiling throughout the road.

While crossing these nurseries she saw the same pink flower which was in neighbour's balcony. She started smiling and then she realized that she was smiling earlier too.

She started looking for same flower in other nurseries to understand what's special with this plant, but she couldn't trace it on the go! After couple of nurseries, she left the hunch and started listening to FM song in the car and humming it loud! Many songs came by like "Channa Mereya" "Humma Humma" and Kunal was also humming these songs as "Tana na na na tana nana" and suddenly she stuck at word "Nana" in humming and remembers that same pink flower was at her Nana ji (Mother's father) place and a big smile came across her face.

It was an evocative moment for her, and image of her Nana ji place came into her mind, there was a gate of U shape (Upside down) which was completely covered with these pink flowers, and she used to love that gate in her childhood. There was a swing made out of chair in the backyard, mango tree with multiple ribbon tied to branches and her Nana use to tie ball with long rope to branch, which makes it easy to play even if the kid is alone and many sweet memories which she hasn't thought in long time.

It felt like forgotten or missed memory came out of nowhere and lightened her heart. While coming back from her friend house she insisted to stop at nursery and bought that plant. Kunal had never seen her so prompt to buy specific thing, she normally gets into ifs and buy and other options available but this time she knew what she wanted and only that plant nothing else. IT made him curious about this plant and he asked her; what's so special in this plant and why you seem so happy. She told him the story of whole day and her feeling and Nanaji place and he started smiling and felt happy by seeing her happy. It's placed in the biggest ever flowerpot she has owned. Her husband calls it

Nana ji plant and she feels like peace whenever she watches that plant.

It reminds her lovely time spent during summer break at Nanaji and all other memories which were forgotten while being busy in day today routine and hustle full life.

Somedays went by and summer holiday's was around the corner. They had decided to go out on vacation in Kerala and other nearby states of South India but her daughter was insisting to go to her grandparents in Lucknow . They both were trying to convince her Kerala and said she can go Lucknow during quick breaks of 3-4 days. Seems like this discussion was not getting over , Disha and Kunal decided that they will make the booking for Kerala and Priya will like it once she is on Trip .

Next day Disha asked Priya to water the plants before she gets ready to school and let Disha know if any plant doesn't seem good . Priya went ahead to water the plant and came running to Disha shouting *"Mumma Mumma"* come outside fast, Priya grabbed her mother hand and pulled her towards balcony . Disha was terrified and wasn't sure what to expect , while Kunal also came running in hustle ; when they reached outside they saw that Nanaji plant has so many new leaves and pink flower trying to blossom.

Priya started jumping saying ***"Nanaji is growing, Nanaji is growing "*** , they started smiling and took a family photo with plant . Disha opened her whatsapp and tried to apply that photo as her profile photo; During that moment she realised that she is loving to have these memories around but not thinking about Priya's time and love with her grandparents which will be happy memories for her in future .

Disha felt that both (Kunal & Disha) are being selfish thinking about their vacation and not taking Dish to her grandparents . Disha spoke to Kunal and they did booking to visit Lucknow this summer and surprised Priya with the booking .

Disha was thinking that how lucky they are to spend that time with loved one and have these memories for life, Nowadays we travel to different places whenever get time but doesn't know how to spend time with loved one. It felt like we all have been running behind things which always need to have some achievement or something tangible linked to it but not about emotions or feeling or love.

_ Usha _

Learnings on the way

It was November. I woke up with a heavy heart on a Monday morning after a long weekend, and it was heavier today since this is the time when annual reviews are typically held . While still lying in bed and scrolling through notifications, thoughts about previous year discussions clustered in my mind. I gathered all my energies and started getting ready for work.

I left home around 8, following my regular timing and route. My thoughts were still clustered. It takes about 30 minutes to reach the office. I am very familiar with the route, traffic, landmarks, stops, etc. on the route, and my mind has nothing much to do. I usually listen to some calm country music on my way, but today I did not. Thoughts about the review kept my mind busy - Am I missing out on any of my accomplishments or rewards? How to pitch in about all the hard work that I did throughout the year? As I approached a big intersection and was ready to cross, the signals turned red. I pulled on the brakes. Additional wait time of a few minutes irritated me.

Beggars and poor kids sell stuff like pens, trash bags, and many things 24/7 at this junction. I saw one boy walking towards my car. He splashed water over my front screen and started cleaning it. In a few seconds, he came sideways and knocked on my side window, asking for money. I got frustrated, opened my window, and shouted at him. He persistently pleaded for money - "Give me 20, Give me 10." I shouted at him again as I waited. I had not asked him to clean my screen.

I finally gave a hard look, closed my window, and started again. He did not react, but I saw his face turn sad. I resumed my chain of thoughts as I drove.

My review with my boss was scheduled post-lunch, and I was well-prepared. I entered the meeting room with a smile on my face, and the discussion kicked off. It was an hour-long discussion, and my boss seemed to be happy with all my efforts but thought that the outcome could have been better. I had kept him apprised throughout the year on how things were going, and he seemed to be aligned and happy, but not today. Today he highlighted all the gaps which he was expecting me to close. I had put in huge efforts and worked for extended hours as well to achieve the best possible. But it did not make my boss that happy. He shared his feedback, which was not as good as I thought I deserved. Probably, I did not do what was expected from me throughout the year. I did not react, but he could have seen my face turn sad. I remembered that morning boy who did something that was really not asked for.

As I returned after a long day at work and came back to the same signal, my eyes kept searching for that boy. I could not find him. I thought I should have asked for his name, but then the signal turned green. I moved, but my heart kept on thinking. Finally, I parked my car safely and walked around to find him. I handed him a 100-rupee note and thanked him. He was not willing to accept, but I held his hand and handed it over.

I did not wait to see the reaction on his face and drove back home.

_ Vikrant _

The Shining Light

The sun is out, birds are chirping, my dog is running around the ground which is wet and little dirty, my mother is at garden humming old Hindi song (Gunguna rhe hain bhaware khil rhi hai kali kali), all windows and doors are open and morning sunlight is entering the house as every place is shining with lights. Seeing all these my face light up with smile and I feel happiness and joy, I didn't take few seconds to come out of bed (usually it takes 10-15mins every day).

It felt like I want to jump straight into my chores and live to the fullest. It's been almost a month we had seen sun as its rainy season and every day we see cloud or rain and desperately waiting for sun. My heart felt light as peace has come to life suddenly and i also starting humming with my mother (Gunguna rahe hai bhawre khil rhi hai kali kali).

My kid is still having sound sleep and I wanted to wake him but knew he will be cranky and wouldn't want to come out of bed and it will be waste of time and mood; instead, I head towards kitchen and thought to make black tea for myself. While my tea was getting ready, I started playing with my dog who was super happy to see me up so early.

I took my tea and grabbed a book to go through few pages as a good start of my day. This book was all about knowing yourself, being present, keep your thinking hat on and etc. Now, the biggest question was where to sit in calmness. if I sit near my mother we will start talking and book & calmness will leave aside. If I stay in dining hall then my dog will not leave me without playing, I can't go to bedroom as my Kid might woke up. The only place left was balcony with flowers and view of sun which seems perfect. I sat on balcony with my book and tea but couldn't take away my eyes from how everything was shining; flower, kids playing area, birds chirping and flying around trying to say morning to sun and feels like sun is speaking its heart out to everything, clearing bad /negativity from world and putting positivity around, feeling everyone with clear thought.

My chain of thoughts doesn't seem to end on this topic. I touched many topics like a flower at podium is so good and we should get one , why leaves looks so green, how many days it will take to dry the ground , Is my tea good or it could have been better , i need coffee maker , my dog is stupid sometime, should i get another dog , what should i eat today , i want to wear which meet my vibe today and many more thoughts and i reached a thought that daily we were seeing so many clouds in Sky and today Sun is talking his heart out to us which made me thought that we also have so many thoughts with in our heart and sometime we don't even try to clear it out . It was so good when we were kids, we use to speak what we think and need or want.

I remember many times talking truth on subjects which people doesn't want to admit and I could do that as there was no fear of how other feels, what other think of me, is somebody going to get offended, I am talking out of line , its none of my business or may be its not my place to say anything . It made me think when it all started and why did I stop being that way. By now there are many questions which had occupied my mind.

I was totally confused and trying to rethink when the last time was i had my heart empty. There is always something I wish I would have said but didn't due to adult thinking. Many times, situations and people move ahead but our heart feels heavy as we didn't say what was needed.

It really moved me to do something about it and I thought to try this again but with some precaution (Adult Thinking).

Where do I really want to implement this? I thought family is a safe start to implement or try this but on other hand I knew that family always supports, and I might feel its work but actually it's not. Next is my office where I spend 8-9 hours of my day, but I have to be careful from where to start. I can't be loud out with everyone but starting with my manager felt a good comfortable spot. For some people it might be scary, but I felt it right as someone once told me that Manager is one person who can make you or break you. He/she might not be the highest position of Company but a very Important person to block or open door for you.

I started making move towards it and consciously spoke when the stake wasn't so high like telling my friend that his behaviour in particular places is bothering me. Openly stated if I did not want to visit some friends or people and all small things. On other side, I started speaking openly with my manager on topics which were important to me like am not interested in particular Work (earlier I would have said Yes to work as No is not the right word) or it might take longer than expected revert time due to challenges or my personal commitment and small things on daily basis.

I am sure you must be wondering how it went as most of us are in this day-to-day routine and want to say all these. It was really difficult to act that way and get away from adult thinking of not worrying about others or not thinking about consequences. I tried as much i can and there were few things which didn't go well (I cannot control others adult thinking) but I was surprised to see how most of it fell in place. My relationship with friend, colleague, family became more stronger as we started being true and being practical and I could be me with them. My manager started knowing my working style and my interest of area, I started saying no to things I am not able to do or I can't do for any reason and my guilt of not fulfilling started decreasing and increased our mutual understanding. I started making time for myself by saying i do not want to participate in few things am not interested in something and life became so easy. Now I feel light and happy every time with less worries.

"Don't be afraid to Speak from heart" – Picturequote.com

_ Usha _

Battlefield

He could feel the heat of the scorching sun and hear the loud shouts of warriors around him in the battlefield. He could see a massive army from the enemy camp coming closer and closer. And with every single step, the little fear he had was turning into rage. His thoughts were coming to a halt. He couldn't feel the weight of his sword and shield anymore. They were too close now. He saw the front row entering the fight and blades started clunking all around. Soon he was standing in front of a tall warrior who was out of control with anger. Shielding himself with his left and finding a spot to hit with his right. That tall man took a second more to retract his sword and .... Tic-Tic-Tic.

He pressed the switch on his old clock. It was 2 am. His brain was still heavy with those thoughts.

He paused for a while and gazed outside. He could see a calm bluish shade of the night sky and a bright full moon. It was peaceful and silent …

Kept his pen, closed the book he was writing and fell asleep.

_ Vikrant _

Unthinkable

Its back 30-40 years ago where it was all male dominance and girls were not given chance the way should be given. Everyone tried to suppress their voice and didn't gave much chance to fly according to their wish or dream. In mid of this era there was a girl born in small village of India, she was the youngest one with 2 siblings. She had very different vibe than any other girl, she will fight to play outside in the field with her brothers and cousins. She would not stay with girls for inhouse games, but she would do what chores are needed in return to get her demands completed. She never thought herself less than anybody, she had courage to go out and say that loud to anybody in-front of her.

Her family was full of soldiers (grandfather, Father, uncles) and had little strict rules but was open minded to give rights to ever individuals.

Her brother used to study in English school and she with her sister was asked to go to Hindi school but she refused to go and cried for multiple days to get into English schools and only aspire to be in English school was to wear tie, skirt and write with pencil, on other hand in Hindi school it was no Tie, suits as dress and ink pen to write with. Her grandfather said let her study for this year and then will change and that's how she got her way to English school.

She always knew what's at stake and she performed really well and became best of the class, her family couldn't take her away as school provided fee concession to keep her in school. She always wished for better things and her imagination was never restricted to her village. She wanted to fly and reach far from where she was.

One day she was attending marriage of her far cousin and her uncle just teased her that your marriage will be like this, and she said 'NO' it won't be same. It will have more stars and colours and flowers and specially very few people, not the whole Village like now. She had never seen a marriage like that, but she had thought of everything more beautiful and colourful. Then her uncle asked her how your groom would be, and she said he will know how to make food, how to clean clothes, how to take care of her, respectful and all other things which none of the boys were doing those days.

Her uncle aunt all laughed and said looks like you are going to marry servant not husband, without thinking a second, she replied it means aunties and her cousins everyone is servant not your wife. Everybody got silent and This incident became an issue of how she behaved and outspoken in front of everyone but her grandfather took her side and told everyone, you all are the one who gave her definition of a servant and nothing wrong on her side. her grandfather had complete faith in her that she is special and will do something different in her life. He was an aspiring person to have in that era.

She grew up and got into job far outside then her village and she started meeting new people and got fascinated by Punjabi culture as they seem to pretty cool, less restriction, happy going and always had thought to get married to someone of that culture.

Whenever she gets into relationships, she always looked for person she wished to get married and any connection of Punjabi culture. She met many people, but nothing worked out. She started searching for groom and met multiple people and by now she had lost hope of getting husband she wished for Punjabi connection. she was going with flow and started looking for compatibility to settle down.

she met on guy and started talking to him and after couple of days of talking she was thinking on how compatible he looks and suddenly she realized that he is all what she had always wished for. He knew cooking, he was kind, he was respectful, he knew all chores and stated upfront that he would like to remain same and doesn't want his wife to do all chores. She jumped out of the bed and couldn't sleep whole night thinking about how it could be true and did not want to let him go in any ways. She was okay him not being from Punjabi culture as she couldn't believe that she got everything except being Punjabi in this guy.

Next day she called him and started getting more involved and trying to know more and more about him to make final decision. During discussion they landed up on culture and if all goes good how it would be, and he mentioned that he is not from Punjabi culture (which she knew) but his both sisters are married into Punjabi and his family had adopted Punjabi culture and it would moreover Punjabi wedding. Her happiness was on cloud nine and she pinched herself to make sure she was not dreaming all this. She has never been happy, thrilled, excited and all confused at same time.

She asked him to meet her mother and let's take this further. Both families met and the day arrived when they set the date.

She got married surrounded with 50 people, which was very unusual but that's what she always dreamt of.

Let your dream fly, let it go where it takes you, hope and wish for what you really want. You never know when they might come true.

_ Usha _

www.ingramcontent.com/pod-product-compliance
Lightning Source LLC
La Vergne TN
LVHW041105150826
845673LV00007B/1938

* 9 7 9 8 8 9 2 3 3 0 9 0 9 *